1 2 3
Little Donkey

By Rindert Kromhout & Annemarie van Haeringen

GECKO PRESS

shopping bag

Look what Mama's bought!

2

nosy friends

What's inside?

3

bags of treats

"Look, Little Donkey!" shouts Bobby.

4

pleading eyes

"Please, Mama? Just one each..."

5

kitchen shelves

"They won't reach them up here."

6

flowers in a vase

"Careful, Little Donkey!"

7

steps on the ladder

,

"Got them!"

8

hooves flying

"Uh-oh!"

9

fat tears

"Mama!!!"

10

soft kisses